No AR

Invitations to Personal Reading, Set B
Curriculum Foundation Classroom Library
Scott, Foresman and Company

Realistic Stories	
Blue Canyon Horse	Ann Nolan Clark
The Bus Trip	Eleanor Frances Lattimore
Chie and the Sports Day	Masako Matsuno
Judy's Journey*	Lois Lenski
Otis Spofford	Beverly Cleary

Biography and Historical Fiction	
Buffalo Bill	Ingri and Edgar Parin d'Aulaire
Copper-Toed Boots	Marguerite de Angeli
Crazy Horse: Sioux Warrior	Enid LaMonte Meadowcroft
The First Book of the Early Settlers	Louise Dickinson Rich
Lee, the Gallant General	Jeanette Eaton

Fun, Fancy, and Adventure	
Basil of Baker Street	Eve Titus
Dorrie and the Weather-Box	Patricia Coombs
The Dwarf Pine Tree	Betty Jean Lifton
Miss Osborne-the-Mop	Wilson Gage
The Perfect Pitch	Beman Lord

Books of Information	
About Policemen Around the World	Les Landin
Mr. Peaceable Paints	Leonard Weisgard
Spike, the Story of a Whitetail Deer	Robert M. McClung
Rusty Rings a Bell	Franklyn M. Branley and Eleanor K. Vaughan
Wonders of an Oceanarium	Lou Jacobs, Jr.

Books Too Good to Miss	
Adventure at Mont-Saint-Michel	Napoli
Favorite Fairy Tales Told in Germany*	retold by Virginia Haviland
Miss Happiness and Miss Flower	Rumer Godden
Once Upon a Horse	Arnold Spilka
The World Is Round	Anthony Ravielli

*Not included in sets for distribution in the British Commonwealth (except Canada).

CHIE AND THE SPORTS DAY

By the same author

A PAIR OF RED CLOGS

TARO AND THE TŌFU

CHIE

THE WORLD PUBLISHING COMPANY CLEVELAND AND NEW YORK

Special Scott, Foresman and Company Edition
for the **Invitations to Personal Reading** Program

AND THE SPORTS DAY

by Masako Matsuno

Illustrated by Kazue Mizumura

Some Japanese names and words you will find in this book:

Chie, pronounced *tchee-eh*
Ichiro, pronounced *ee-tchee-ro,* means *first boy*
Niichan, pronounced *nee-ee-tchan,* means *older brother*
Sushi, pronounced *soo-shee,* means *rice cakes*
Mamagoto, pronounced *mah-mah-go-toe,* means *playing house*
Yo-o-i! Don!, pronounced *yo-ee dohn,* means *Ready! Bang!* or *Ready! Go!*

Published by The World Publishing Company
2231 West 110th Street, Cleveland 2, Ohio
Published simultaneously in Canada by
Nelson, Foster & Scott Ltd.
Library of Congress Catalog Card Number: 65–13416

This edition is printed and distributed by Scott, Foresman and Company
by special arrangement with The World Publishing Company.

"Why should we take her? It's no fun to play with a girl,"
Michio said to Ichiro.
"I won't play with you if she goes with us," said Hiroshi,
and the two boys ran away.
Ichiro looked back at Chie for a moment,
then he too ran after the boys.

Chie rubbed the tears from her eyes and watched the boys disappear.
Bright dragonflies flew around her head in a friendly way,
but Chie was lonely.

Chie kicked a stone, and then another.
The stones rolled merrily, chasing each other.
But Chie had no one to chase.
It seemed she was always alone these days.
Kicking stones, Chie went home.

Before, Ichiro had often played *mamagoto* with Chie.
He had pretended to eat the food Chie made with leaves and flowers.
And Ichiro took Chie with him on butterfly hunts.

But everything changed when Ichiro became a schoolboy.
He no longer played *mamagoto* with Chie.
Now, every day after school, Ichiro played with his school friends.

Once in a while, not very often, Ichiro took Chie out to play with him,
and they raced. But soon,
"Crybaby, you're too slow," Ichiro would say, clicking his tongue.
And he would run away to join his friends, just as he had today.

Chie opened the kitchen door slowly.
"Chie? Is it you?" Mother called, hearing her footsteps.

But Chie didn't answer. She didn't want to see Mother.
She knew just what Mother would say.
"Don't cry, Chie. Ichiro will play with you tomorrow."
Always, she said the same thing, but tomorrow never came.
Chie knew it wouldn't.

"Chie?" Mother called louder. "Come in, Chie, and taste this."
Chie opened her eyes wide in surprise.
There on the table were sandwiches, cakes,
bananas and apples, chocolate candies, *sushi* . . .
"Is it a picnic?" Chie asked.
"No."
"A party?"
"No."
"What? What are these for?"
"Sports day!" Mother said merrily.
"Sports day?"
"Yes. Ichiro's sports day at school tomorrow.
Didn't he tell you about it?"

"No, nothing. Can I go?"

"Yes," Mother answered, busily cutting more sandwiches.

"You and I are going tomorrow."

"Tomorrow! Oh, tomorrow!" Chie cried, and skipped for joy.

Ichiro, too, was surprised to see the splendid lunch
when he came in from play.

"It's for sports day tomorrow," Mother explained.

"But why three lunches?"

"One for me," said Chie excitedly.

"And for me too," Mother added, smiling at Ichiro.

"But you said you couldn't come! You said you had to attend
an important meeting!"

"Yes, but I'll cut it short. It's your first sports day.
I want to be there," said Mother.

"And me too," Chie cried.

Ichiro looked at Chie.

Then, without a word, he turned and ran to his room.

The whole house shook as Ichiro slammed the door
and threw himself on the floor.
Chie was coming to the sports day.
No, he couldn't bear it.
It will be awful, Ichiro thought bitterly.
She will see me running last. Last!

Always, when Ichiro and Chie raced together, Ichiro won.
"Ichiro-*Niichan* is so fast," Chie would say admiringly.
But at school Ichiro was almost always the slowest runner of his class.
Chie did not know it.
Ichiro didn't want Chie to know it.
He wanted to keep it secret.
He didn't care if anyone else knew he was a slow runner.
But not Chie.
"She shouldn't come," said Ichiro, thumping his feet.
"No, she shouldn't. Oh, I hope Mother can't get there in time."

Sports day was a beautiful autumn day.

The music of the opening march soared into the deep blue October sky,

and under the gay buntings girls danced.

"All first-grade boys! Fall in at the starting gate,"

called the teacher of athletics over the microphone.

"Please, please . . ." Ichiro prayed to himself as he took his place.

"Don't let them be here yet."

His eyes searched the crowd. No, he didn't see them.

Goody, they couldn't make it! Ichiro smiled secretly.

The first-grade boys were divided into groups.

"*Yo-o-i! Don!!*" (Ready! Go!!) The first group ran!

"*Yo-o-i! Don!!*" The second group ran!

Now!

"*Yo-o-i! Don!!*" The third group ran! Ichiro ran!

Ichiro forgot all about Mother and Chie.

He ran as he had never run before.

But soon everyone in his group was ahead of him.

He was slow as usual.

"No matter," said Ichiro to himself, running.

"No Mother, no Chie, no Mother, no Chie . . ."

The yellow tape for the next group was already up when,
his heart beating fast, he ran through the goal.

"Ichiro-*Niichan!*"

"Ichiro!"

Mother and Chie! They had just come in!

"You were the first, *Niichan!*" Chie called to her brother.

"No! Last!" Ichiro shouted.

"Last?" Chie was puzzled.

"Yes! Last!"

And seizing his lunch box Ichiro ran away to join his friends.

During all of lunch time, Ichiro stayed away from Mother and Chie.

The obstacle races began in the afternoon.

Anyone who chose could join these games.

Barrels, ladders, nets, and other obstacles were placed on the course,

and near the end were scattered slips of paper.

After a racer cleared all the other obstacles,

the words on his slip told him what to do next.

"Get a yellow cap" or "Find a man's shoe" or

"Tie this rope."

Look! People burst into laughter.

Over there, a fat man was caught in a ladder.

He began running with it around his stomach.

Ichiro enjoyed obstacle races.

It was nothing for him to creep under a net or crawl through a ladder.

He picked up his slip of paper.

"Find a little girl and run three-legged with her," it read.

"Chie! Chie, come quickly!"

Ichiro stopped right in front of Chie's seat.

"What is it? What's wrong?" asked Mother in a worried voice.

"I need a little girl to run with me three-legged."

"*Me?* Not me?"

"Yes, you!"

"Oh yes, I'll go with you!" Chie ran to her brother.

"Hurry, hurry, Ichiro-*Niichan!*"

Ichiro quickly tied his right foot
to Chie's left foot with his head band.
One, two . . . one, two . . . Carefully, the two started.

Now, faster!
One, two; one, two; one, two; one, two; one—

Ah! Ichiro stumbled and fell, dragging Chie with him to the ground.

Red blood ran on her knees.

"Oh . . ." Ichiro exclaimed. Now they would be out of the race.

Chie would cry and run back to Mother.

"Hurry! Let's go! *Niichan,* please hurry!"

Chie pulled Ichiro's hand.

Together, Chie and Ichiro ran. One, two . . . one, two . . .

Left, right; left, right . . . One two; one two . . . They ran and ran.

And it was not until he was untying their feet at the end of the course
that Ichiro realized they were first.

"Tra-ra-ra . . ."

The music began again, and Ichiro and Chie walked together proudly
to receive the first prize.

It was only then, at the retiring gate,
that Chie noticed her bloody knees.
Tears welled up in her eyes.
"Come," said Ichiro.
He carried Chie on his back to the nurse.

"Does it hurt?"
"No, not much."
Outside, the sun seemed even brighter than before.
Ichiro walked slowly for Chie's sake.
"You won. You won first prize!" said Chie, looking up at Ichiro.
"I? No, we!" Ichiro replied, smiling.
"Half of the prize is yours.
Take these notebooks and pencils.
And you can have the whole box of crayons."
"Really?"
"Yes, really."

Chie was very, very happy.

"Look, Mother," she called. "My notebooks, my pencils.

And a whole box of crayons!

I ran with Ichiro-*Niichan,* and we were first."

And Ichiro was happy too.

Why?

Because he won first prize, of course.

But not only because of that.

Can you guess why?

"Tra-ra-ra . . ." the music was still playing.

Ichiro skipped to the music to meet his friends.

It was a beautiful autumn day.

A deep blue October sky and bright, golden sunshine.

Bang! Bang! Up went the firecrackers. Bang! Bang! Bang!

The games went on.

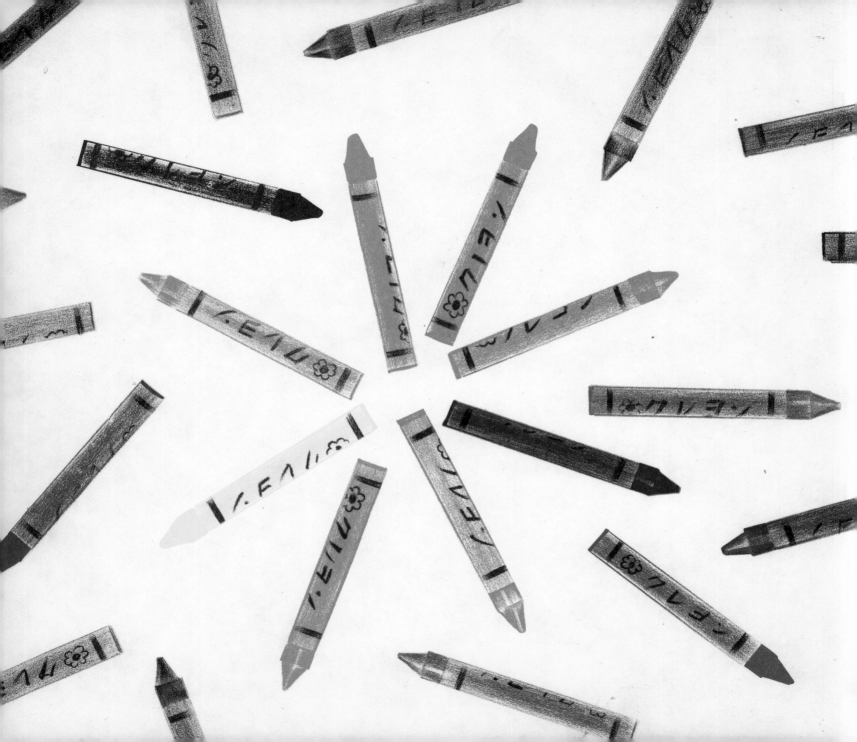